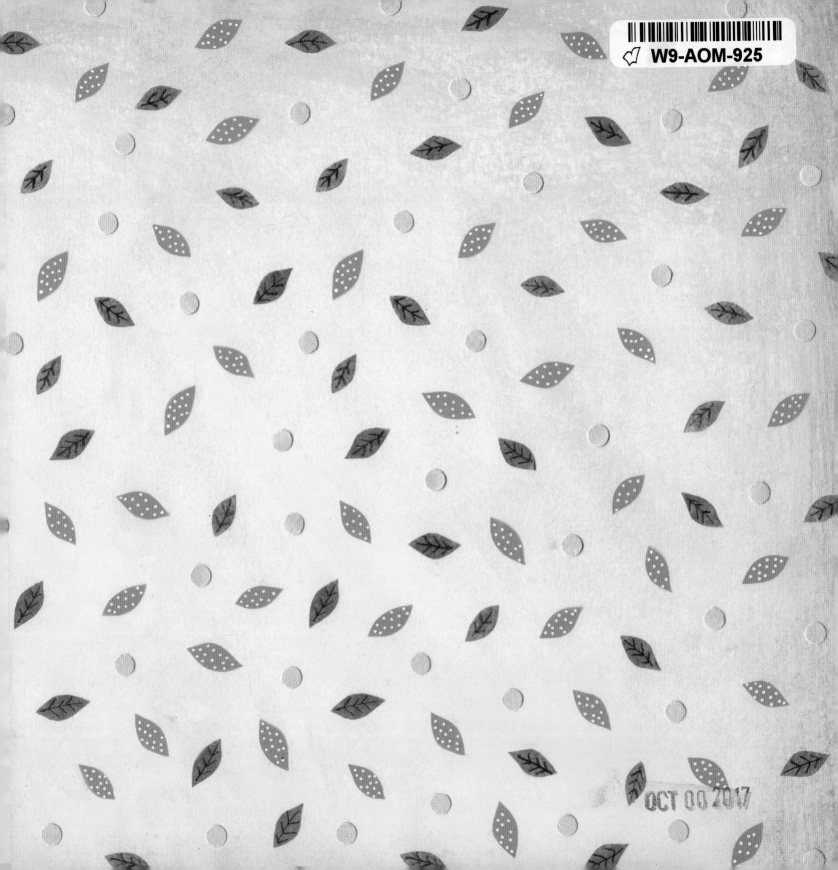

**The Mirror in Mommy's House /
The Mirror in Daddy's House
Somos8 Series**

© Text: Luis Amavisca, 2016
© Illustrations: Betania Zacarias, 2016
© Edition: NubeOcho, 2017
www.nubeocho.com – info@nubeocho.com

Original title: *El espejo en la casa de mamá / El espejo en la casa de papá*
Translators: Kim Griffin and Ben Dawlatly
Text editing: Caroline Dookie

Distributed in the United States by
Consortium Book Sales & Distribution

First edition: 2017
ISBN: 978-84-945415-5-1
Printed in China

THE MIRROR
in Mommy's House

Luis Amavisca
Betania Zacarias

nubeOCHO

It was so long ago that I can
hardly remember,
but there once was a time
when I had only one house.

Back then, in that single house,
Daddy and Mommy used to argue a lot.

And it made me sad...

One thing I can remember is that when they argued,
I always used to go and gaze into the mirror.

There, inside, I would imagine many things...
Fantastic voyages and amazing animals.

Now I have two houses:

Daddy's house and Mommy's house.

I really like both of them.

Mommy's house has books all over the place. I love books!

There is a little red sofa and big windows with a view of the park.

Mommy and I play together all the time.
Sometimes we dress up and
the house turns into a spaceship!

Even though the two houses are different, they have some things in common...

In both houses, I have photos of me with Daddy and Mommy.

And there's something that's exactly the same in my bedroom at Daddy's house and at Mommy's house...

A great big mirror that I love gazing into.

Daddy and Mommy love me so much.

They know that they share something magical...

A great big mirror that I love gazing into.

Mommy and Daddy love me so much.

They know that they share something magical...

Even though the two houses are different, they have some things in common...

In both houses, I have photos of me with Mommy and Daddy.

And there's something that's exactly the same in my bedroom at Mommy's house and at Daddy's house...

Sometimes, Daddy's house turns into a
magical jungle filled with plants and spices.

The smells are just wonderful!

Daddy's house always smells delicious.
He loves to cook!

There is a big blue couch and little
balconies with views of the city.

Now I have two houses:
Mommy's house and Daddy's house.
I really like both of them.

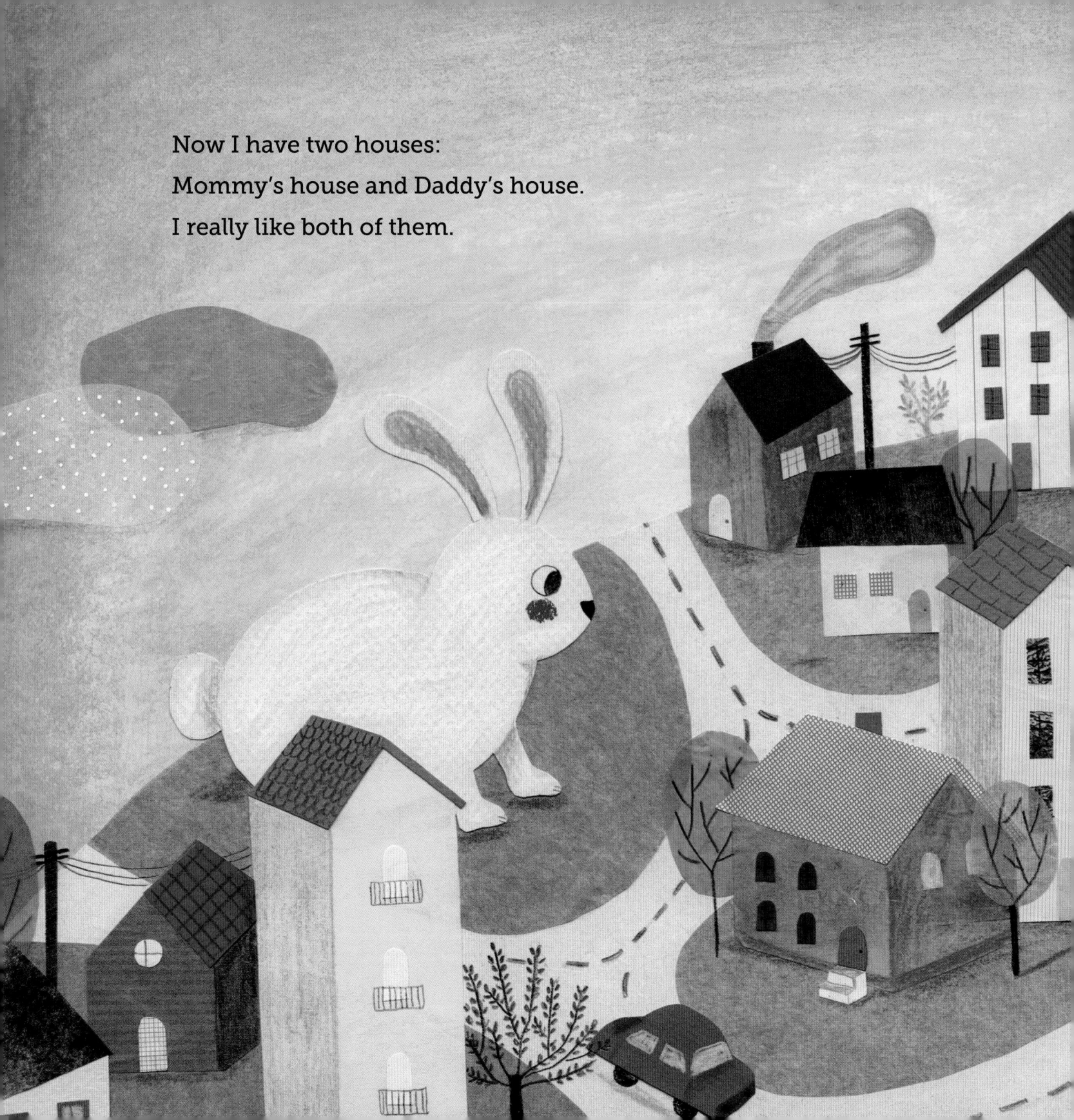

One thing I can remember is that when they argued,
I always used to go and gaze into the mirror.

There, inside, I would imagine many things...
Fantastic voyages and amazing animals.

Back then, in that single house,

Mommy and Daddy used to argue a lot.

And it made me sad...

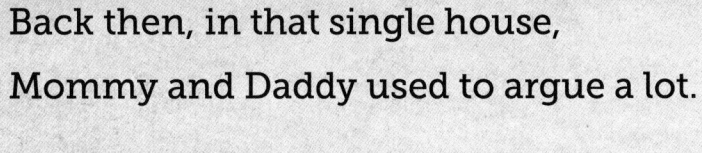

It was so long ago that I can
hardly remember,
but there once was a time
when I had only one house.

nubeOCHO

Luis Amavisca
Betania Zacarias

THE MIRROR
in Daddy's House

**The Mirror in Mommy's House /
The Mirror in Daddy's House
Somos8 Series**

© Text: Luis Amavisca, 2016
© Illustrations: Betania Zacarias, 2016
© Edition: NubeOcho, 2017
www.nubeocho.com – info@nubeocho.com

Original title: *El espejo en la casa de mamá / El espejo en la casa de papá*
Translators: Kim Griffin and Ben Dawlatly
Text editing: Caroline Dookie

Distributed in the United States by
Consortium Book Sales & Distribution

First edition: 2017
ISBN: 978-84-945415-5-1
Printed in China